Feelings

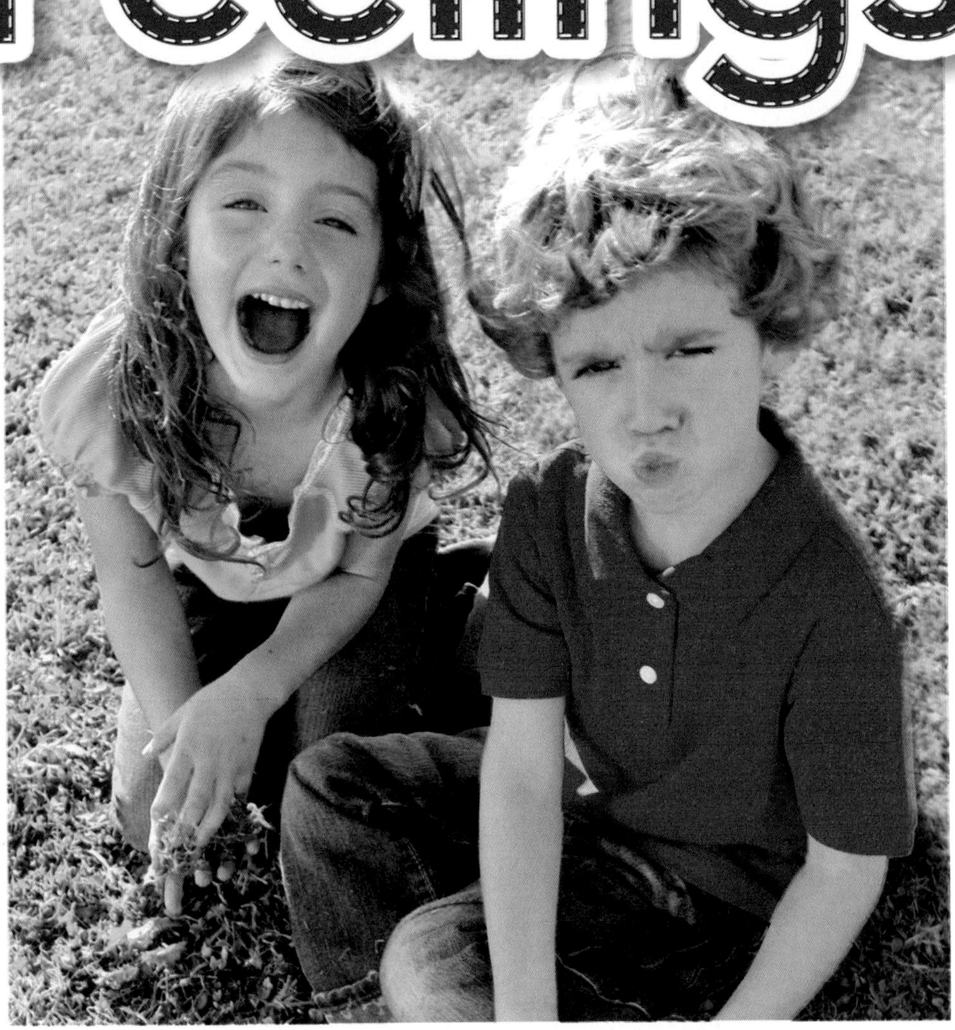

Stephanie Reid

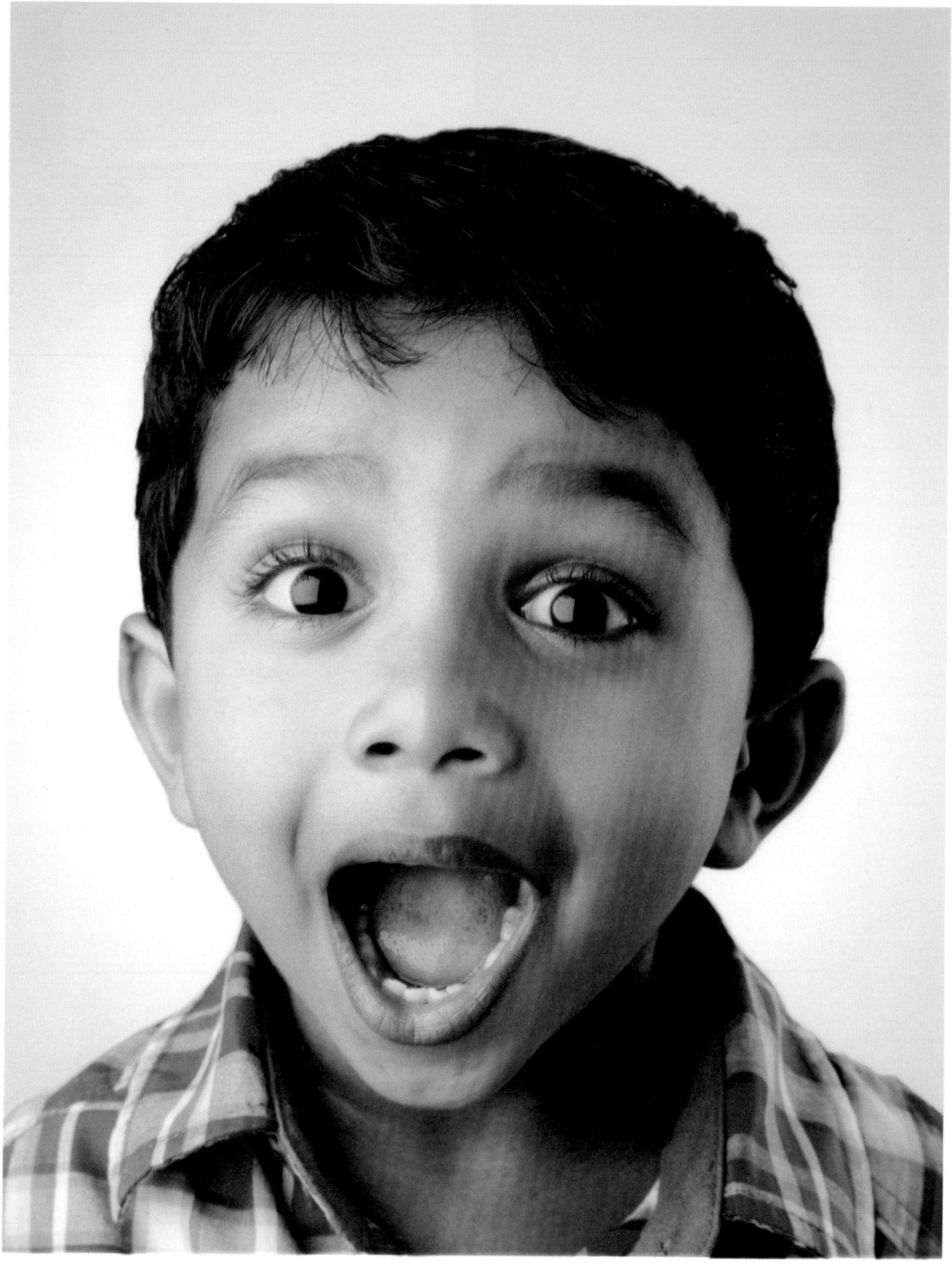

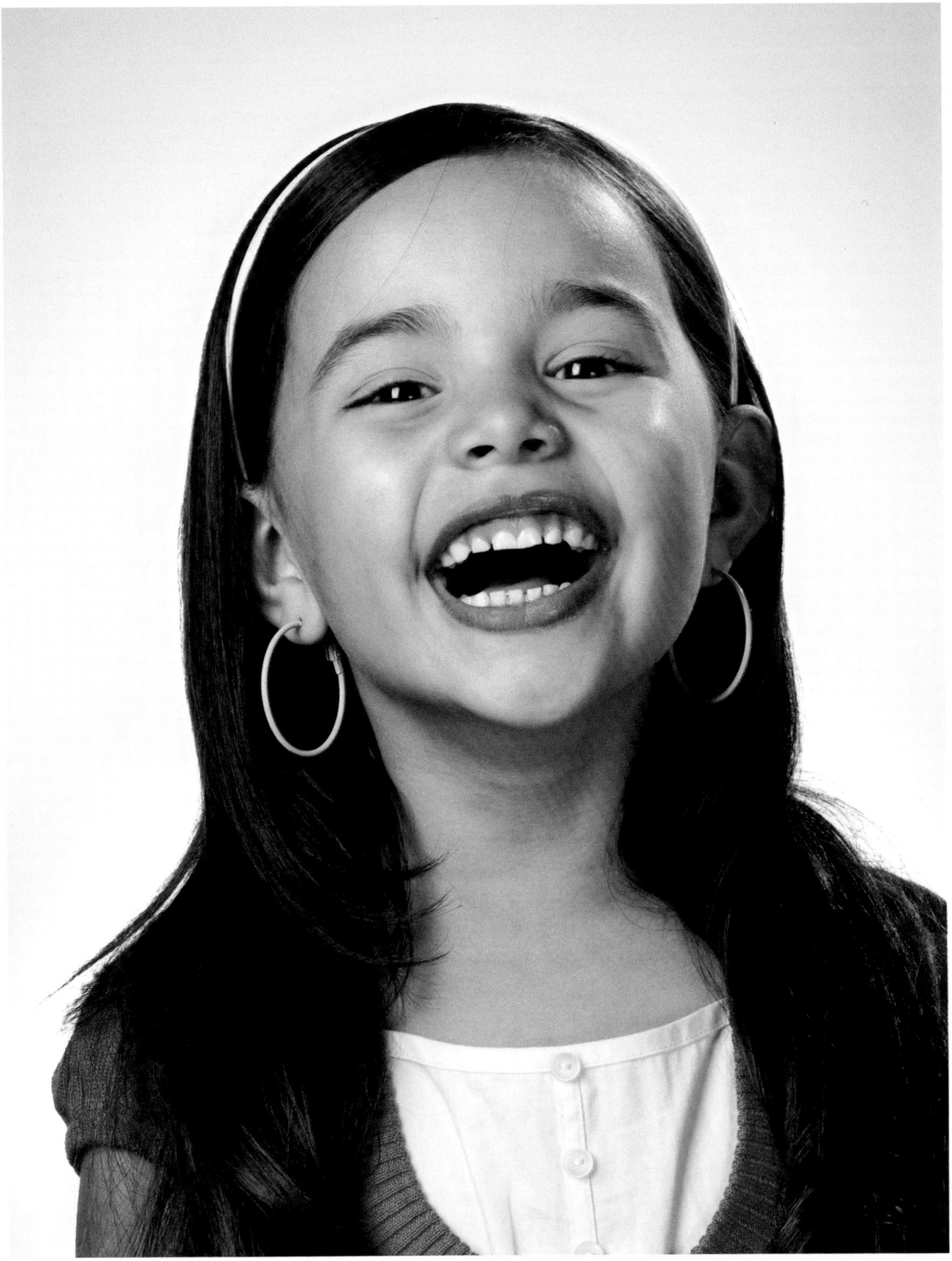

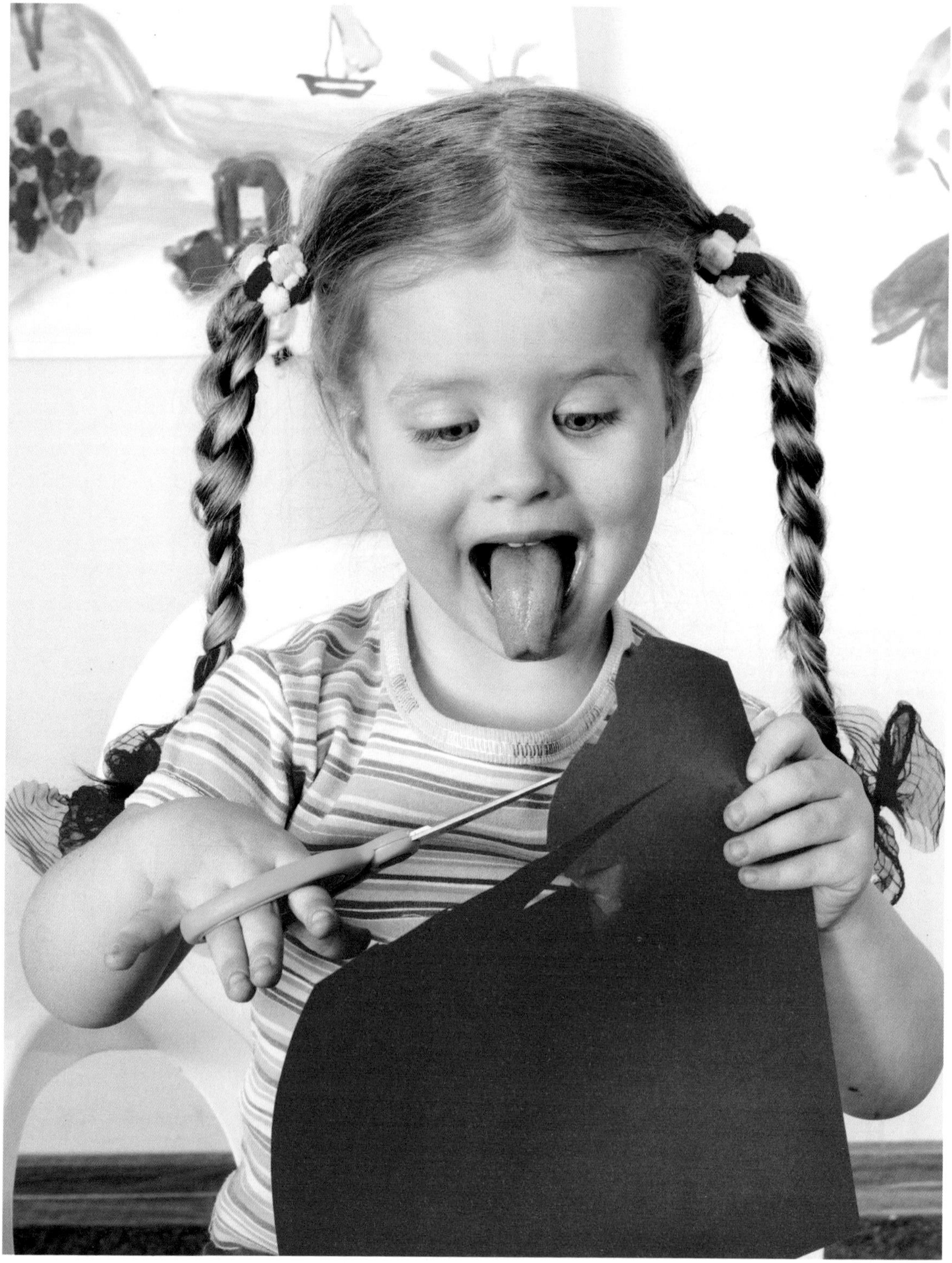

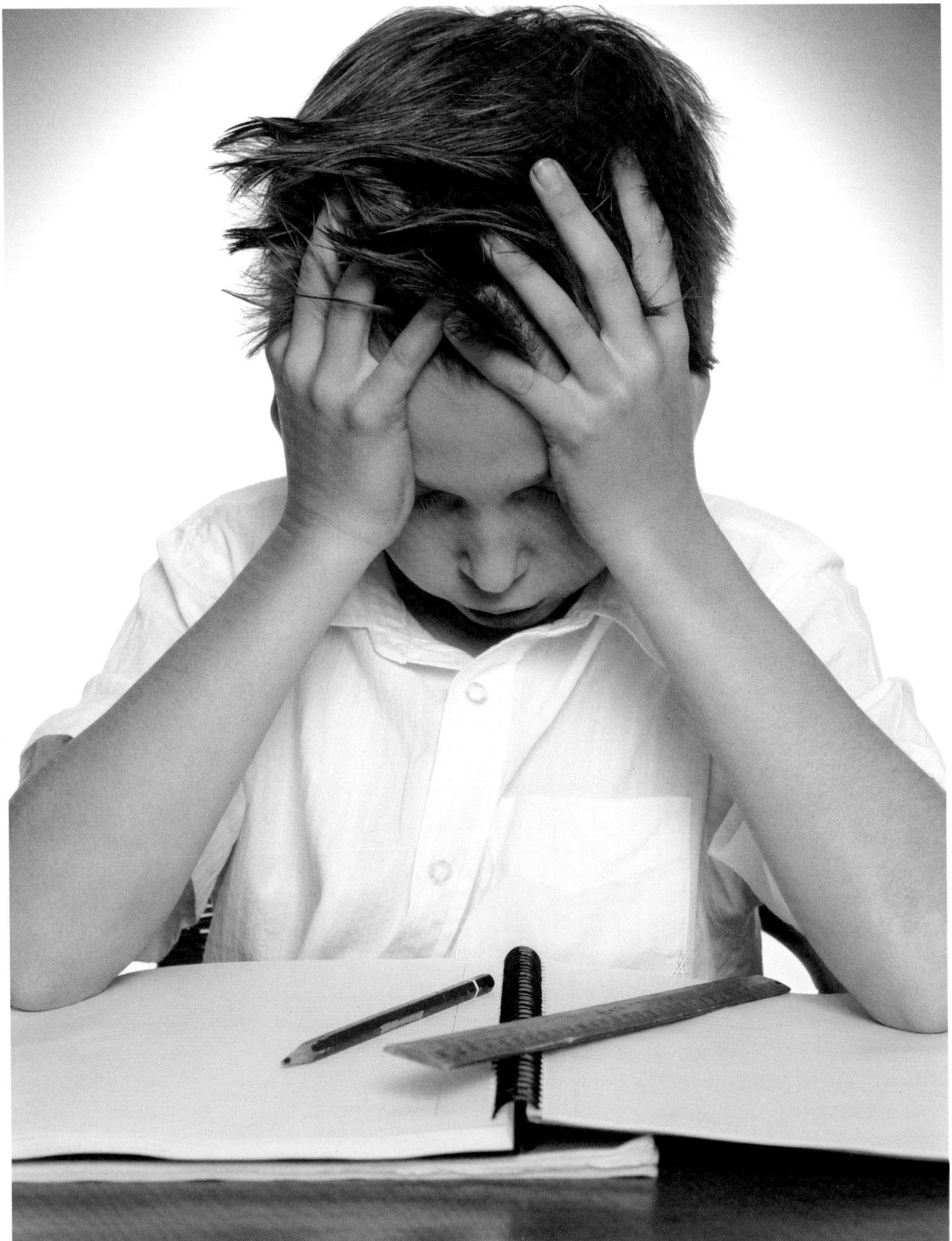

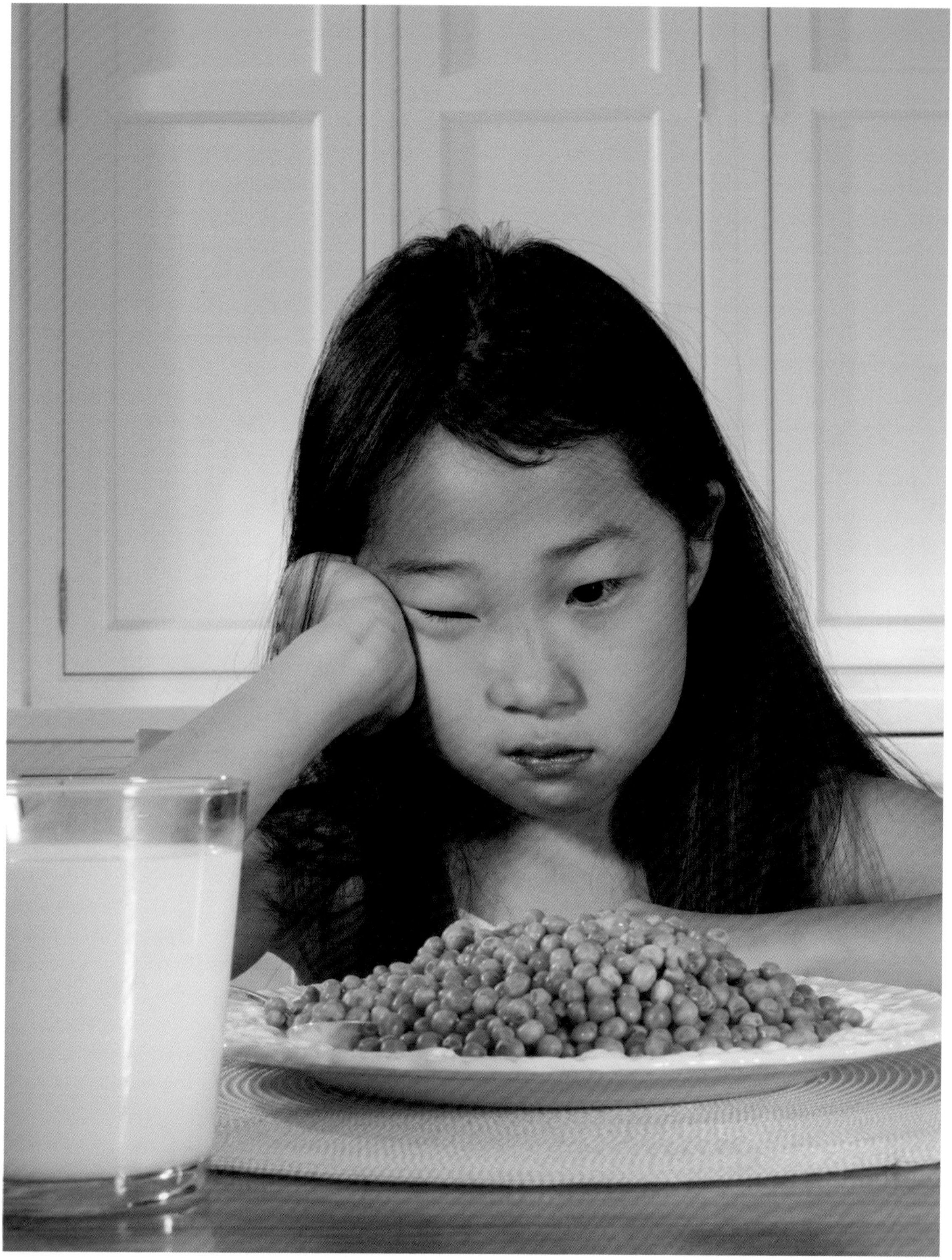

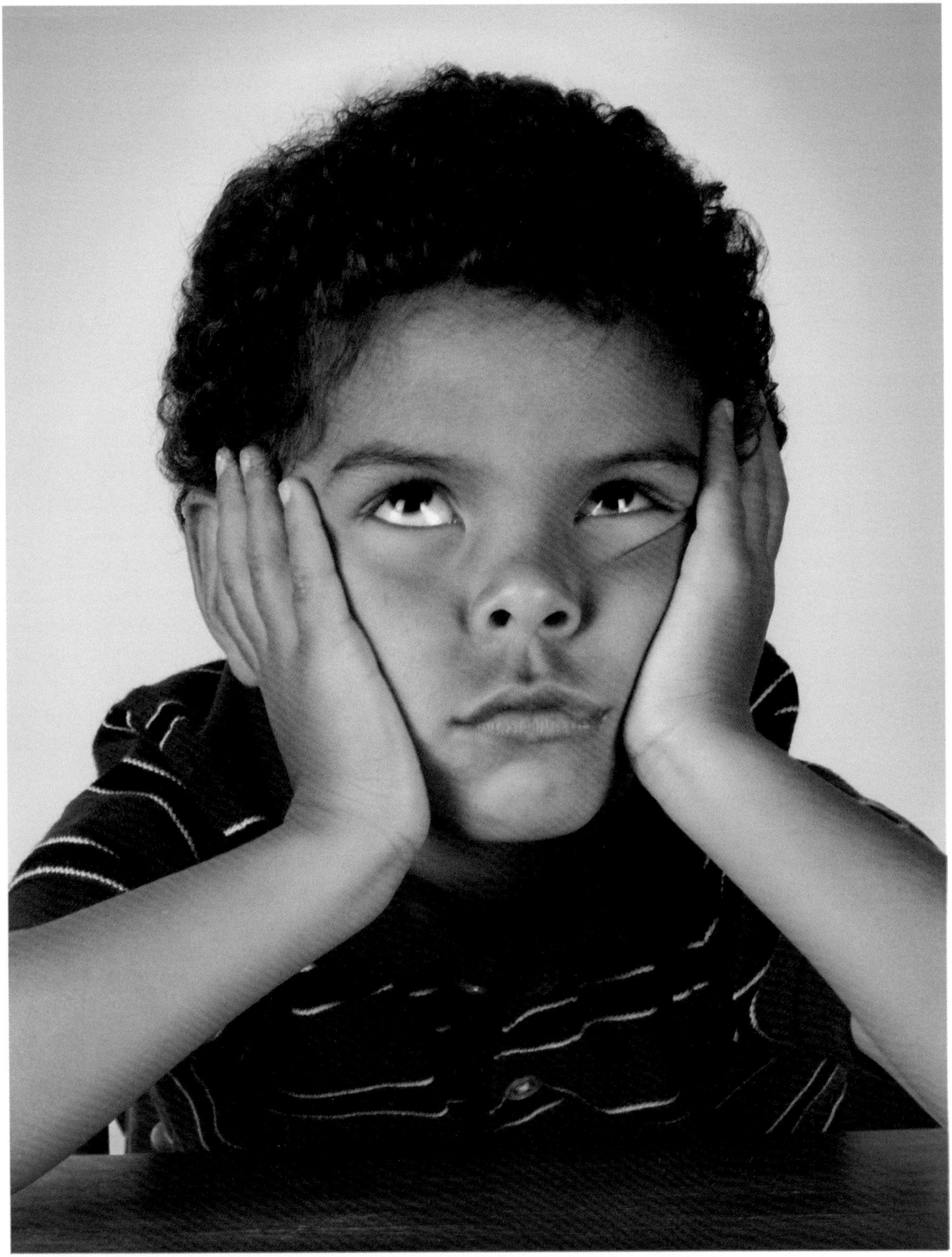

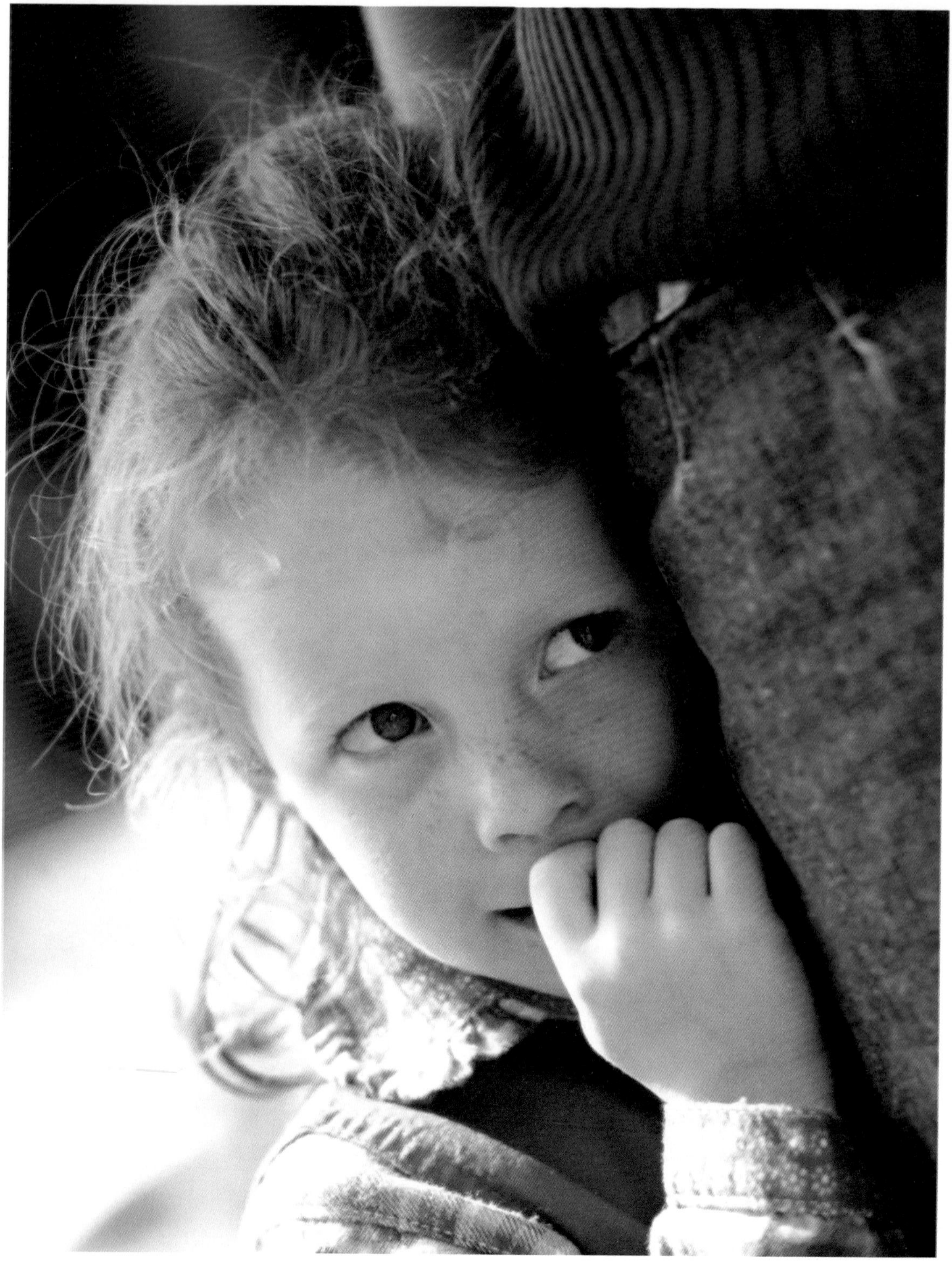

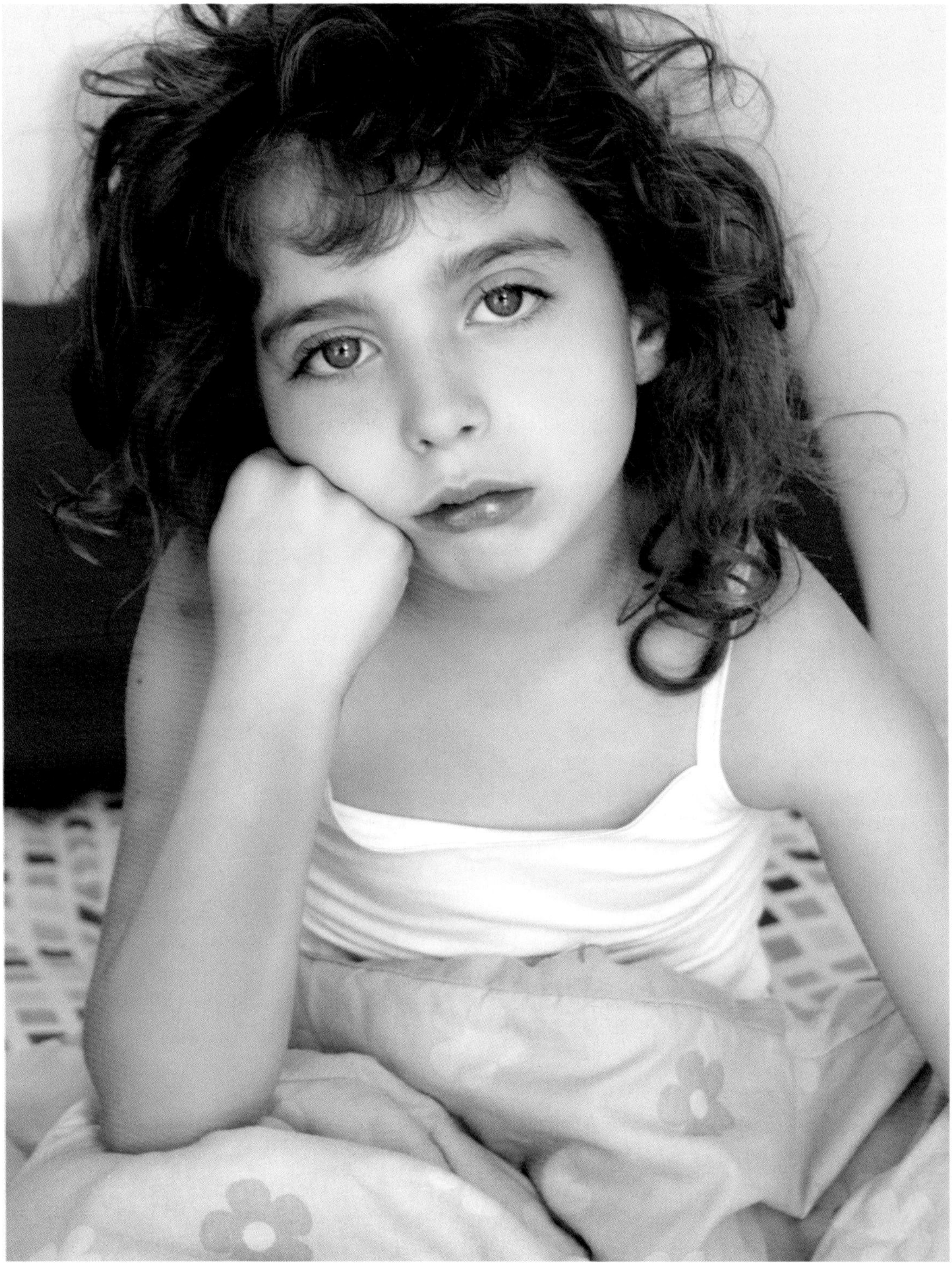

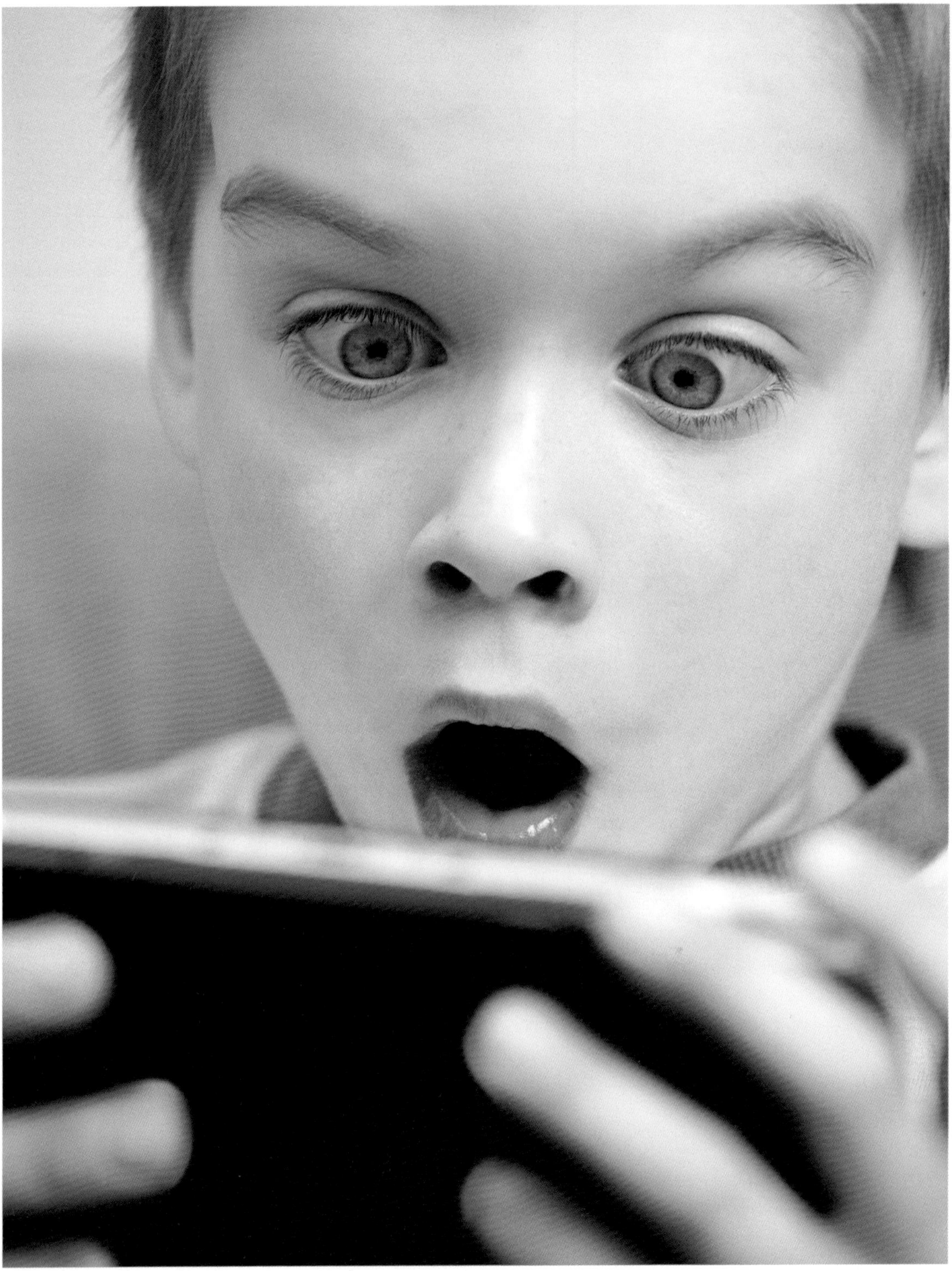

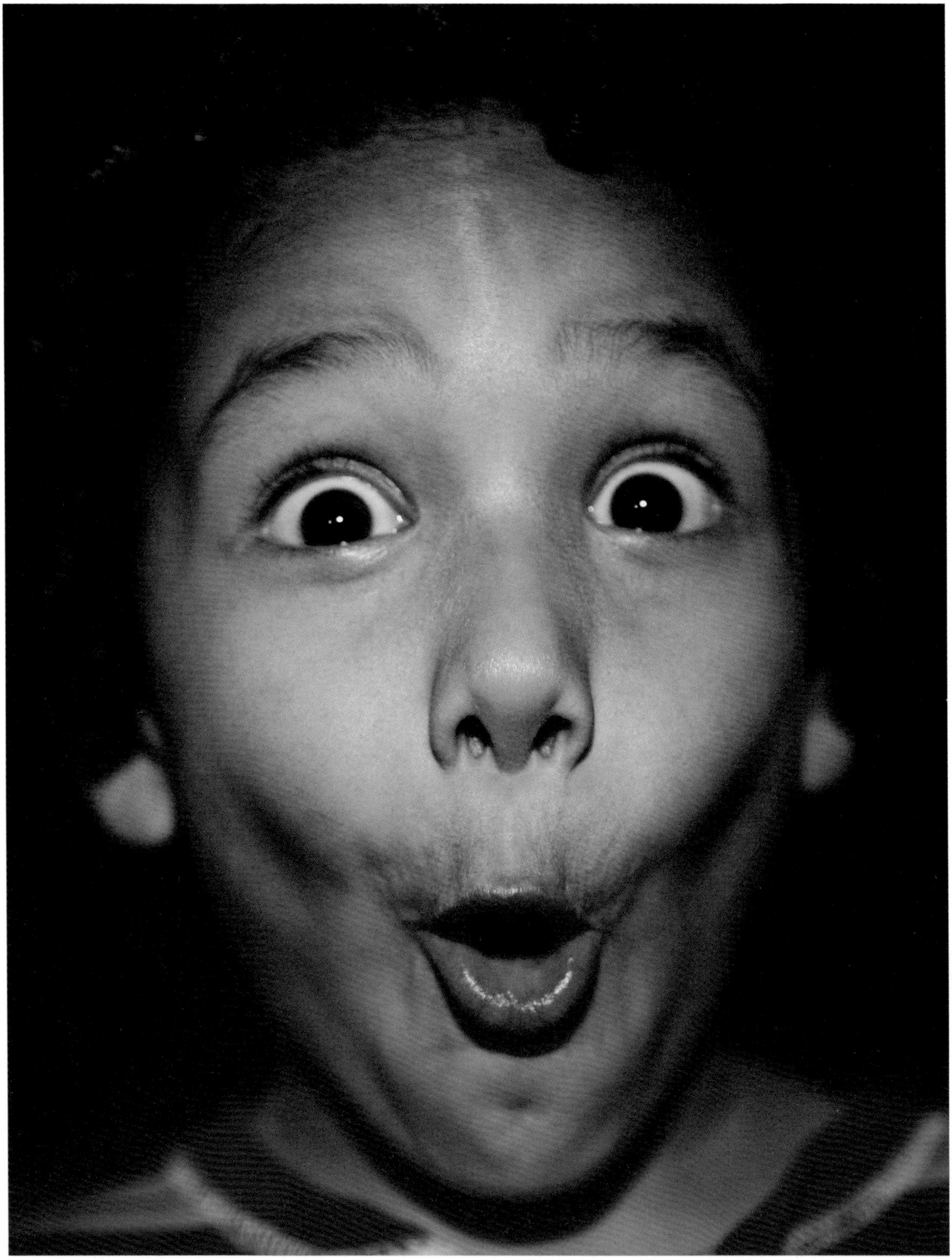

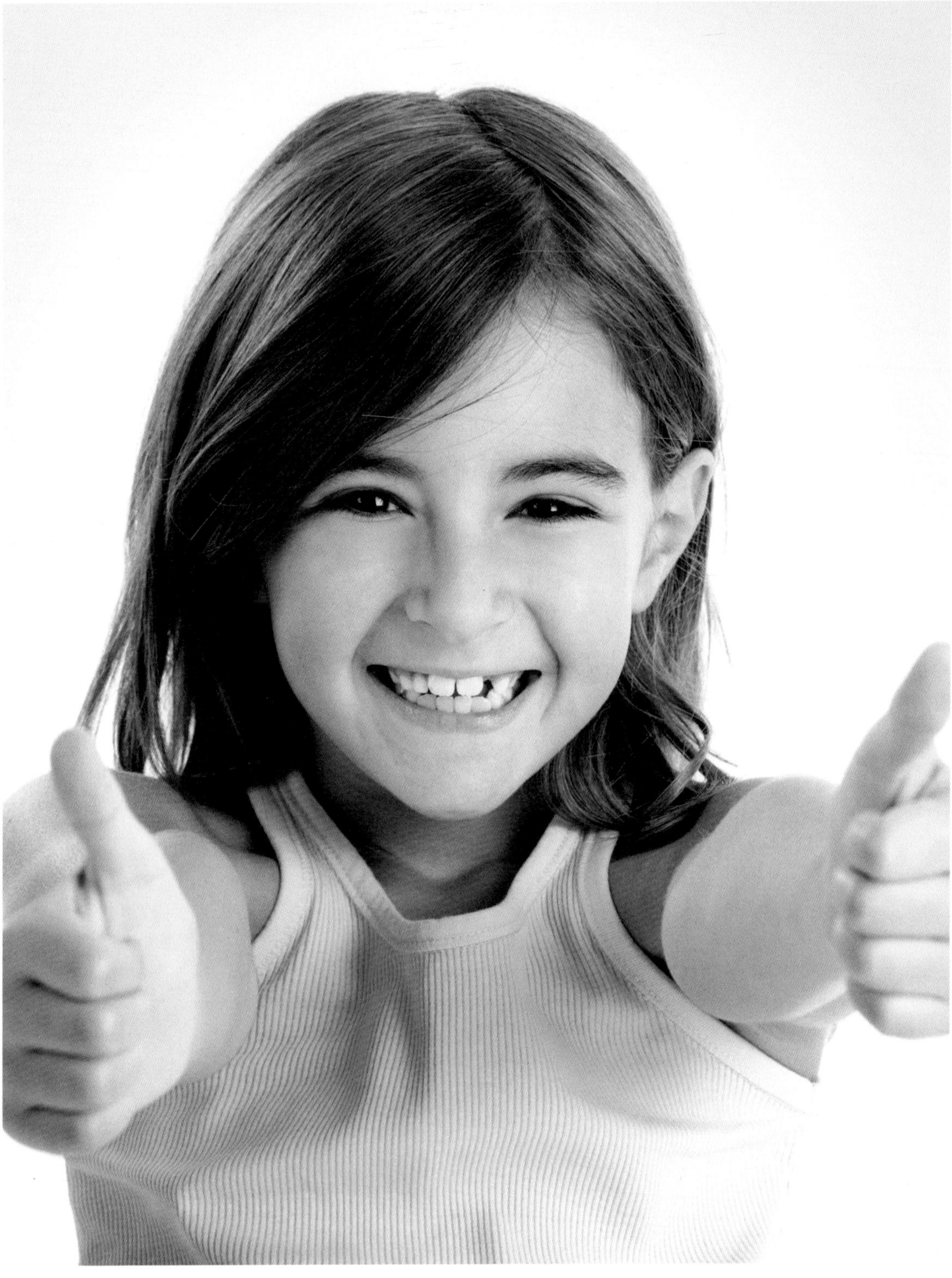

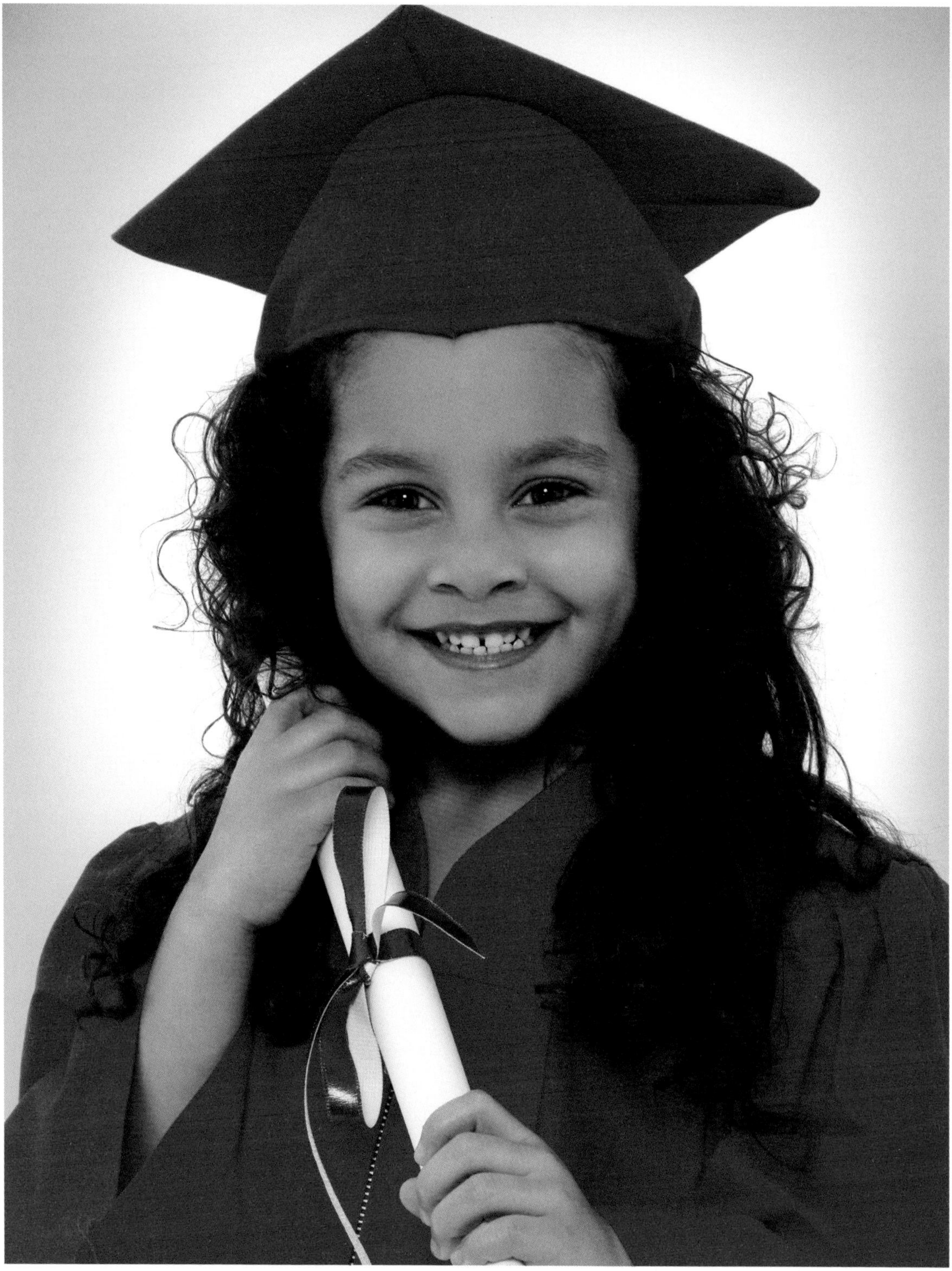

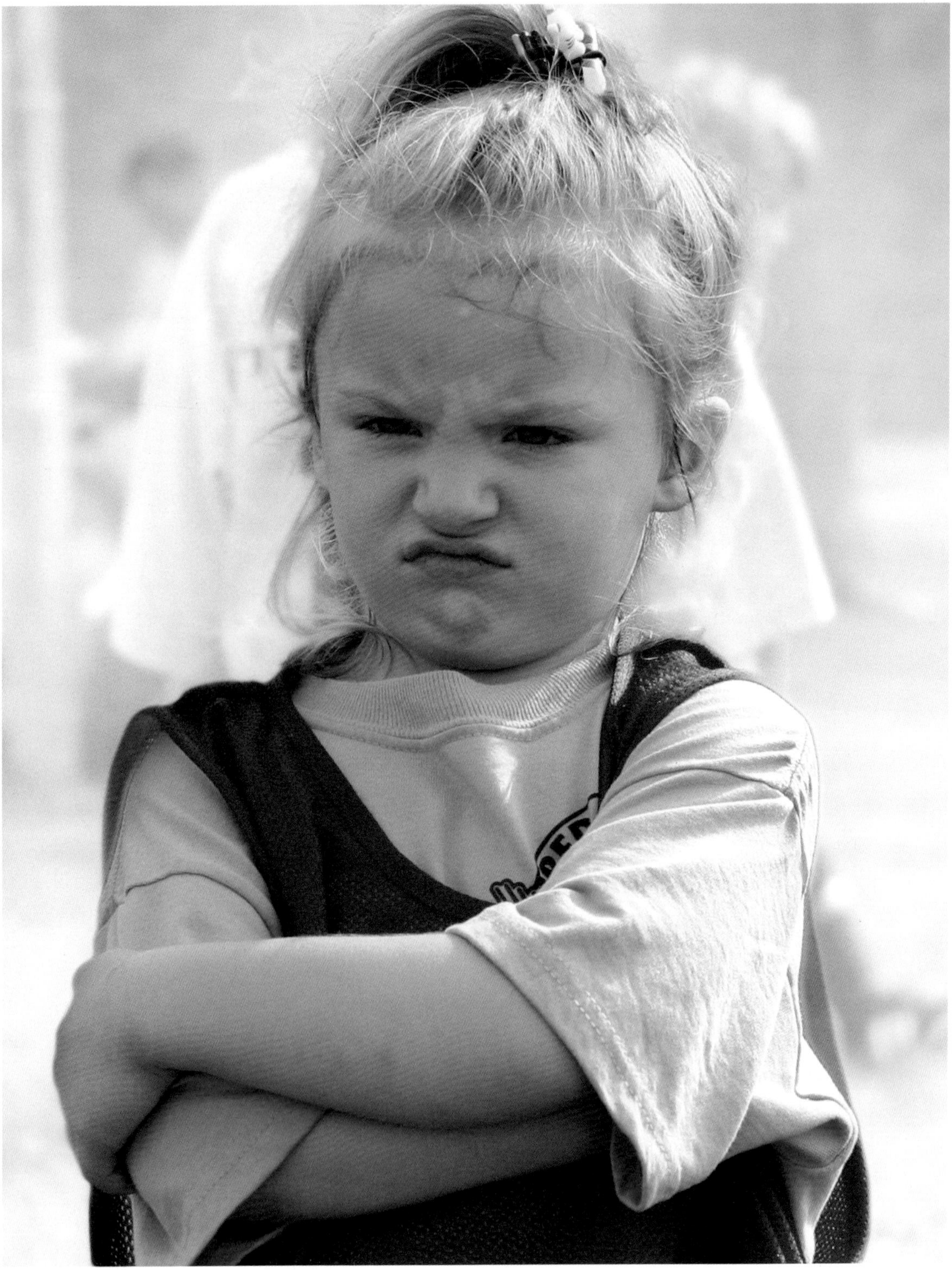

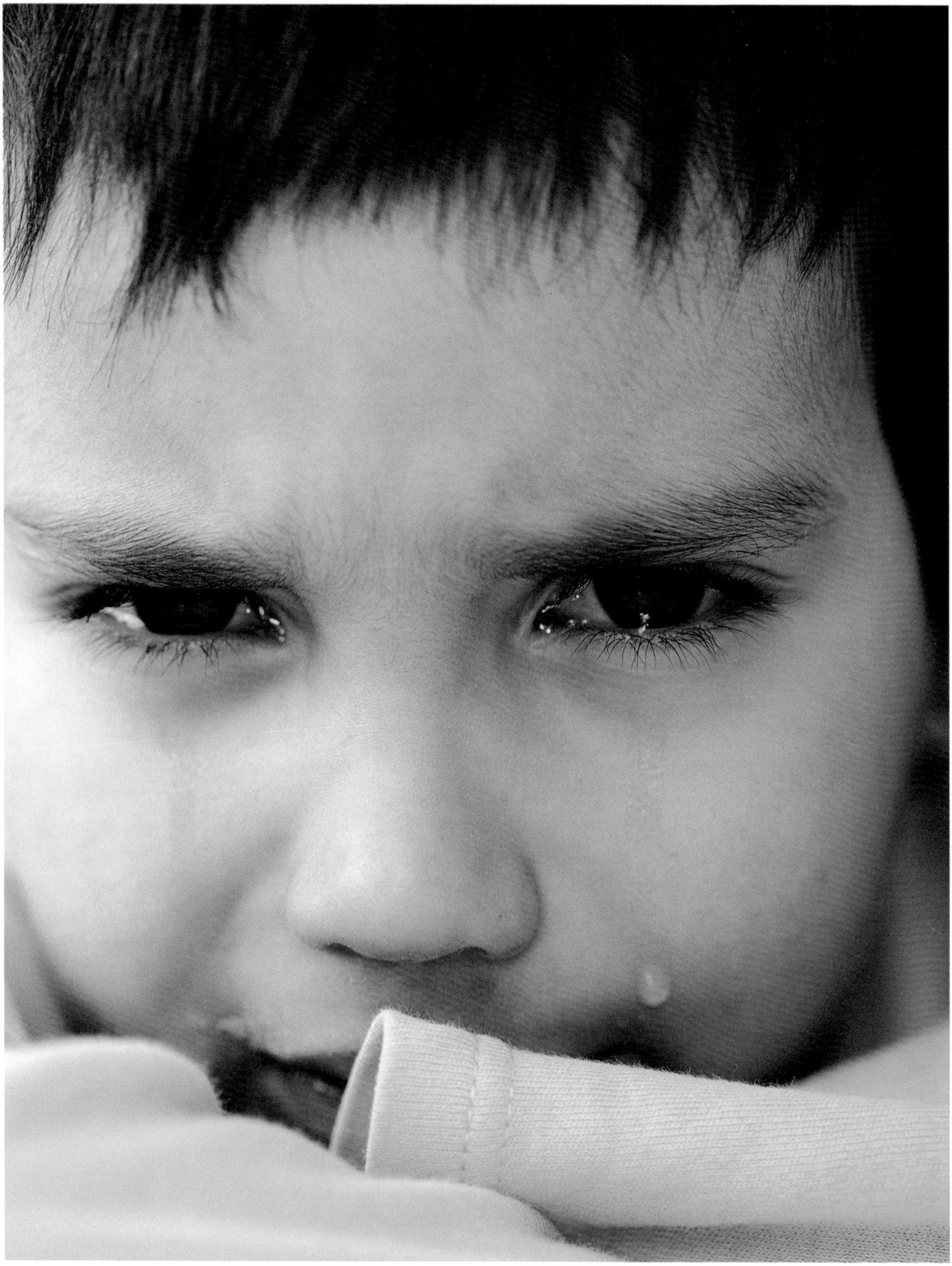

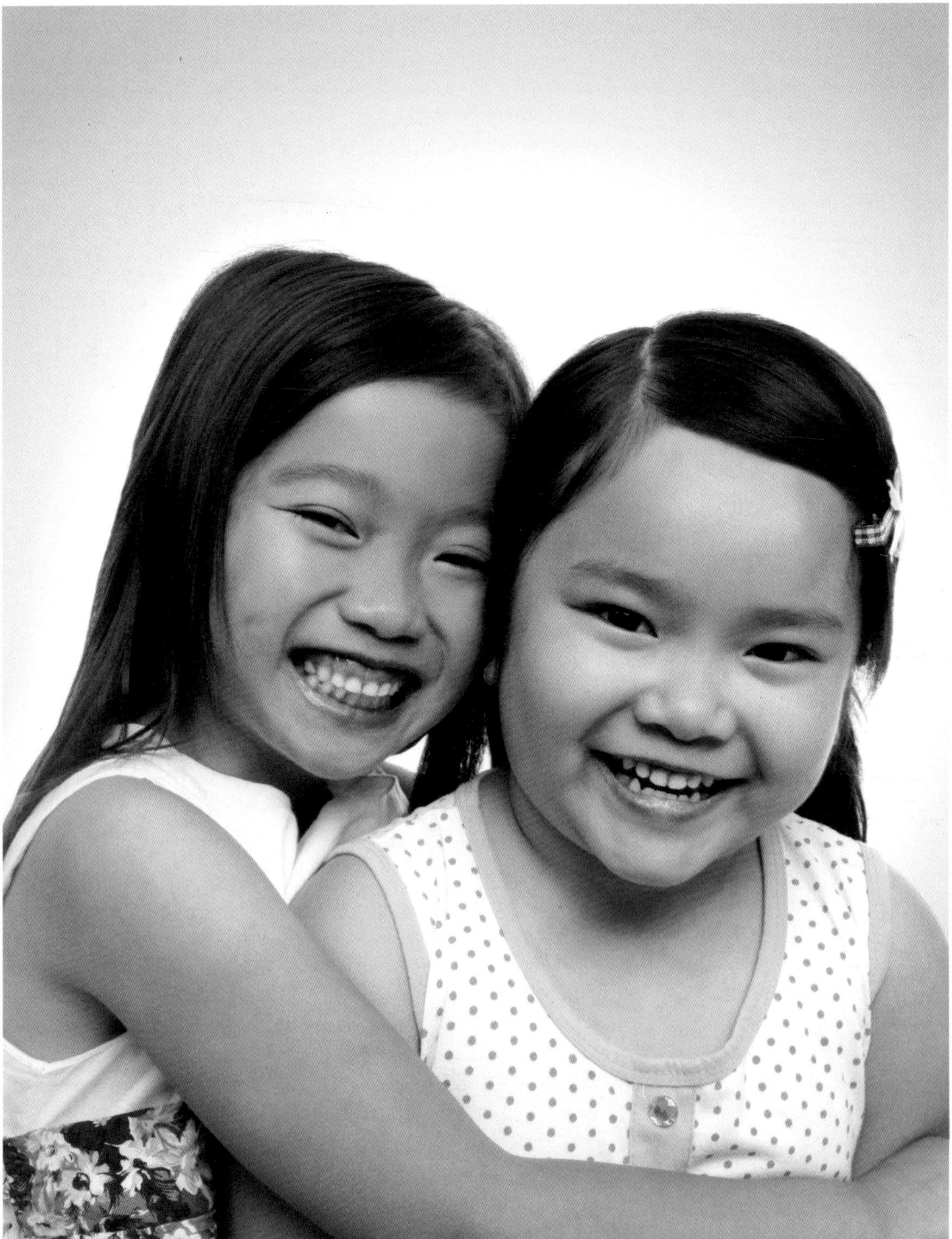